W9-BZB-644

# Stan the Dog and the Golden Goals

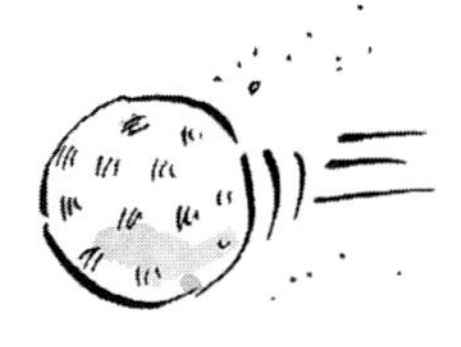

written and illustrated by
Scoular Anderson

PICTURE WINDOW BOOKS
Minneapolis, Minnesota

*For Alexander*

Editor: Jill Kalz
Page Production: Brandie E. Shoemaker
Creative Director: Keith Griffin
Editorial Director: Carol Jones

First American edition published in 2007 by
Picture Window Books
5115 Excelsior Boulevard
Suite 232
Minneapolis, MN 55416
877-845-8392
www.picturewindowbooks.com

First published in 2002 by A&C Black Publishers Limited, 38 Soho Square,
London W1D 3HB, with the title STAN AND THE GOLDEN GOALS


Printed in the United States of America.

**Library of Congress Cataloging-in-Publication Data**
Anderson, Scoular.
Stan the dog and the golden goals / by Scoular Anderson. — 1st American ed.
p. cm. — (Read-it! chapter books)
Summary: Grumpy because he is not allowed to play with the soccer team, Stan the dog gets into a fight, little realizing that super stardom is just around the corner for him.
ISBN-13: 978-1-4048-2740-0 (hardcover)
ISBN-10: 1-4048-2740-4 (hardcover)
[1. Dogs—Fiction. 2. Soccer—Fiction.] I. Title. II. Series.
PZ7.A5495Stg 2006
[E]—dc22 2006005435

# Table of Contents

# Chapter One

Stan the dog loved chasing things. At the top of his list were cats.

But there was a problem with cats. They were very good at getting out of Stan's reach.

There were rabbits at the far end of the park. Stan liked scaring them.

But like the cats, they soon got out of reach. It wasn't very fair.

Sometimes, Stan tried to go after them, but he always got into trouble for getting dirty.

Chasing sticks was better because Stan always caught up with them. Stick-chasing usually happened when the family went to the park. The person Stan called Can Opener never threw sticks.

Crumble couldn't throw sticks.

Big Belly threw sticks when he was in the mood. His aim wasn't very good, and the sticks usually ended up in the middle of the pond ...

... or up a tree.

The best stick-thrower was Handout.

Stan liked chasing balls best of all. He loved the way they bounced up in the air.

Handout liked soccer, so he was always kicking a ball around the backyard.

Stan sometimes played goalie.

Being such a good goalie, Stan was really excited about soccer tryouts. Every day, he jumped up on the kitchen stool to check the calendar.

There was a big match coming up against the Lairdberry Juniors. Stan was sure he'd be asked to play. He might have been a dog, but that didn't really matter. He had talent.

# Chapter Two

The day of soccer tryouts arrived. Handout came home from school and had a snack. Stan took his usual place under the table.

But Handout didn't give Stan a handout.

Stan wandered into the living room.

He leapt up onto the sofa and shoved the cushions out of the way.

He found a few cookie crumbs,

a couple potato chips,

and a half-eaten energy bar.

Finally, he tried the armchairs, too. He found only a small, plastic tube.

Stan had to wait for Handout to get ready. Just to make sure he wasn't forgotten, Stan stayed by the door.

Stan got a shock when Handout finally got to the door.

Then Big Belly walked over.

Stan was horrified.

He was desperate to get out the door.

# Chapter Three

Mr. MacTackel, the soccer coach, was about to start the match.

The match started. Stan took a big interest in the game.

Stan couldn't stand it any longer. He leapt forward, and the leash slipped out of Big Belly's hand.

The boy with the ball was lining up his shot ...

... but in three leaps, Stan was near the goal.

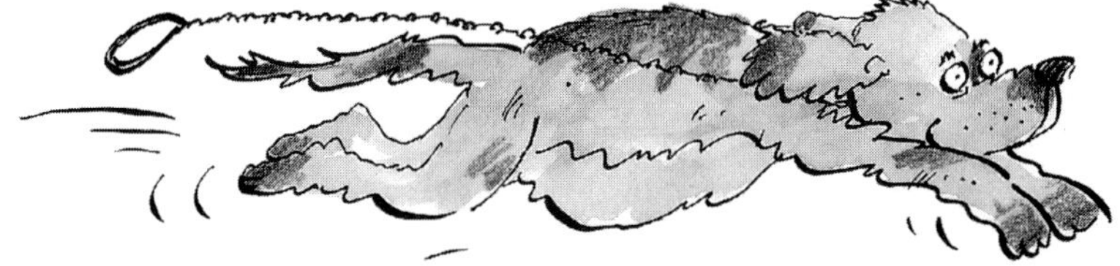

The ball flew ...

... and Stan dove.

The ball shot up,

Stan shot back,

and the goalposts collapsed.

Handout was very upset.

Big Belly went over and apologized to Mr. MacTackel.

Mr. MacTackel blew the final whistle. Everyone went inside for refreshments. Handout was still furious with Stan.

Big Belly tied Stan up with the leash.

# Chapter Four

Stan sat and wondered what was happening inside the field house.

At that moment, a snack fell out of the sky.

Then the owner of the French bread came out of the sky, too.

The bread was a bit big for the crow to pick up easily. Stan thought he could steal it away.

But each time Stan moved forward ...

... the crow managed to jump just out of his reach.

Around and around the soccer field they went.

Just as Stan made a final leap, the crow grabbed the bread in its beak and flew off.

Stan was in for more trouble when everyone came outside.

Big Belly had tied Stan up to the chalk machine that was used to paint the lines on the field.

As Stan had chased the crow, he had dragged the chalk machine behind him. The field was now covered in white lines.

Thankfully, Mr. MacTackel was very understanding about it.

Handout *wasn't* very understanding about it.

On the way home, he refused to have anything to do with Stan.

# Chapter Five

Handout had been picked to play for the team, but not as the goalie. He practiced in the backyard every day after school.

Stan wasn't allowed to play. He had to watch from inside the house. Handout still wasn't speaking to him.

Handout grew grumpier as the day of the match drew nearer. On Saturday morning, he laid his uniform neatly on his bed.

Stan wanted to wish him good luck, but Handout didn't want to listen.

Finally, the time came for Handout to go to the soccer field.

Dad will take you in the car with Stan.
Aw, Mom, why does he have to come?
It's OK. Calm down. He'll need a walk after the match.
I'll put him in the car until the game is over.

The visiting team had already arrived at the field.

Their coach looked at the rickety old goalposts.

He stared at the lumpy, bumpy, soggy field covered in white marks.

He grumbled about the field house.

At last, the big game got started. The Lairdberry Juniors were soon three goals ahead.

Stan had to watch the game from inside the car.

Stan
rolled
down a
window,

squeezed out of the car,

and was soon
racing
home
at great
speed.

The back door was still open. Stan ran inside.

He dug out the plastic tube from beneath the chair cushion.

Then he ran back to the soccer field as fast as he could.

The game had stopped for a time-out. Handout was wheezing.

At that moment, an inhaler appeared!

Handout inhaled deeply. After a few moments, he was able to play again. Right away, he scored a goal.

But it was the only goal his team got. They lost, 1-5.

# Chapter Six

Just as everyone was getting ready to leave, a van pulled up by the field. A woman jumped out and walked up to Big Belly.

She showed them a card.

Di Mulligan took a photo out of her folder.

Handout changed back into his soccer shoes to kick balls to Stan for the camera.

# Chapter Seven

A few weeks later, the family sat down to watch "Paws for Prizes."

They were just in time.

On the show tonight: couple of goldfish that waltz together ...
paws for prizes
... and a cat that saved its owner from a fire!
But first, here's STAN ...
He's amazing!
... the remarkable soccer dog!
Not only can he draw pictures of himself ...
We went down to his local soccer field to check him out.
... he's also a superb goalie!

Then there were lots of shots of Stan as a goalie. He didn't let a single ball through.

Stan won, of course. His goal-saving moves proved to be pure gold. His family decided to use the money to improve the local soccer field.

Handout tied his soccer jersey around Stan's neck.

Stan couldn't stop wagging his tail.

Stan got a special snack.

Then the family went out to celebrate in a restaurant. Stan didn't mind being left at home.

# Look for More *Read-it!* Chapter Books

| | |
|---|---|
| *Grandpa's Boneshaker Bicycle* | 978-1-4048-2732-5 |
| *Jenny the Joker* | 978-1-4048-2733-2 |
| *Little T and Lizard the Wizard* | 978-1-4048-2725-7 |
| *Little T and the Crown Jewels* | 978-1-4048-2726-4 |
| *Little T and the Dragon's Tooth* | 978-1-4048-2727-1 |
| *Little T and the Royal Roar* | 978-1-4048-2728-8 |
| *The Minestrone Mob* | 978-1-4048-2723-3 |
| *Mr. Croc Forgot* | 978-1-4048-2731-8 |
| *Mr. Croc's Silly Sock* | 978-1-4048-2730-1 |
| *Mr. Croc's Walk* | 978-1-4048-2729-5 |
| *The Peanut Prankster* | 978-1-4048-2724-0 |
| *Silly Sausage and the Little Visitor* | 978-1-4048-2735-6 |
| *Silly Sausage and the Spooks* | 978-1-4048-2736-3 |
| *Silly Sausage Goes to School* | 978-1-4048-2738-7 |
| *Silly Sausage in Trouble* | 978-1-4048-2737-0 |
| *Stan the Dog and the Crafty Cats* | 978-1-4048-2739-4 |
| *Stan the Dog and the Major Makeover* | 978-1-4048-2741-7 |
| *Stan the Dog and the Sneaky Snacks* | 978-1-4048-2742-4 |
| *Uncle Pat and Auntie Pat* | 978-1-4048-2734-9 |

Looking for a specific title? A complete list of *Read-it!* Chapter Books is available on our Web site:

**www.picturewindowbooks.com**

MATTAPOISETT FREE PUBLIC LIBRARY
3 2038 00070 8414
OCT 08
Free Public
MAR 2 6 2009
JUN
FEB 1 9 2019
MAR 2 7 2009
JUL 0 7 2009
NOV 1 4 2009
FEB 11
APR 3 0 2016
JUN 2 3 2010
JUL 2 1 2010
DEC 0 7 2010
JUL 2 8 2011